SOUL

YA GOTTA BREATHE

MANNY CABO

BEYOND
PUBLISHING

Quantity sales special discounts are available on quantity purchases by corporations, associations, and others. For details, contact the publisher at the address above.

Orders by U.S. trade bookstores and wholesalers.
Email info@BeyondPublishing.net

The Beyond Publishing Speakers Bureau can bring authors to your live event. For more information or to book an event contact the Beyond Publishing Speakers Bureau speak@BeyondPublishing.net

The Author can be reached directly at BeyondPublishing.net

Creative contribution by Linda Henson
Illustrator - Chris Davey

Manufactured and printed in the United States of America distributed globally by BeyondPublishing.net

BEYOND
PUBLISHING

New York | Los Angeles | London | Sydney

ISBN: 978-1-63792-256-9 Hardcover
ISBN: 978-1-63792-257-6 Paperback

Library of Congress Control Number: 2022901575

TESTIMONIALS

"Manny ignited me and brought me back to a place where everything literally started for me... His electricity and positivity is contagious."
Adam Levine, Maroon 5, NBC's *The Voice*

"It's not often that you find a singer that can tackle great Pop rock music and Manny is a master of it."
Blake Shelton, Country Star

"Manny's got a crazy voice that can make a timeless album and influence the world."
Pharrel Williams, 13x Grammy Winning Artist / Producer / Songwriter / Designer

"Manny Cabo has a voice like butter, a soul full of fire, the grit of a warrior and a heart made of gold... Look out world! It has been an absolute pleasure sharing stages with him and a true honor to be a guest on his podcast: *Mojo For Musicians*!"
Dhomomique Murphy, 3 Time Emmy Winning TV Personality / Speaker / Author

CONTENTS

PROLOGUE

I intentioned many days ago to write a story that would inspire readers who, like me, were walking through life's many hardships, throwing light on the road ahead. I wrote Soul.

I poured my heart out into every page because I owed it to myself to be honest and as forthcoming as I possibly could, to put out uplifting energy to those reading the story and to let them know that they're not alone when faced with, doubt, fear or self- made obstacles.

Understanding humans and our unique journeys can be a daunting task. That's why it's so important to first understand and love who you are before you can love another soul.

I can honestly say that the most eye-opening revelation of my life has been you never truly know where the next leap in your life will come from. Habituate yourself to be in the state of expecting. Put forth the intention of the things that you most desire and expect your dreams to materialize

When you believe you achieve. Be ready for it. Arm yourself with the confidence to tackle whatever obstacles lay between you and your dream.

Much love and peace.

Take a deep breath. Learn to breathe.

Manny Cabo — May, 2022

CHAPTER 1
AND THEN SHE WASN'T

Arabesque, glissade, tour jete. It didn't happen. There was a very loud pop. The audience heard it and was silent. Leslie's left hip was a brick; the pain was unspeakable. A small, quick nod and her understudy was there.

Several hands and arms hustled her off the stage. She couldn't walk. She'd lost her peripheral vision and her hearing was off.

The group was talking.

"Did she slip?"

"I don't think so. I heard a pop."

They thought she'd slipped. There was no slip. Her life was over.

When they let her go to allow her to walk on her own, she sank to the floor. Then they got it.

She heard, "Oh, no!"

Leslie Beaumont was a principal dancer and one of the most powerful athletes in the American Ballet Theater. Right now, she was flailing on the floor unable to right herself.

"Leslie, what happened?" David, her partner's understudy, asked.

"Everything just happened. Everything," said Leslie. "I think my Achilles and maybe something with my back, my hip. The chain reaction. I am dying."

David saw Sergei Orlov, the company magic man, hurrying toward them. Sergei, a muscular six feet, scooped Leslie up and carried her to his room. David headed back toward the stage.

As he lay her on the table and began his examination, he asked, "Leslie, where?"

She could hear the music and was still lost in the sweep of it. She was accustomed to pain, but this was a new dimension, far beyond anything she'd ever known. Instinct told her it was over.

She told Sergei and they communicated in that way that they had with nods, blinks and shrugs. Almost telepathic.

"I see why you say that. Shall we fight back? It'll be hideous."

Sergei understood everything. He had been a rising star in the Kirov when a "pop" had truncated his career. He'd undergone intense rehab for eight months and returned to the stage as an even more powerful dancer. The following year when he had labral tears, he did not return to the stage, so he opted for another profession. He spent five years becoming the one to repair, to encourage and to fix the

dancers. He was a chiropractor, did PT, and did massage. He was patient and usually successful. He always knew what his dancers were facing because he had lived it.

There was massive trauma in Leslie's legs, back and hips. They'd start with cryotherapy, mobilization, and then coaxing massages. They'd have to assess the outcome after each treatment and make appropriate adjustments. Leslie would have to sustain the pain and allow the time.

They had been lovers since she joined the company.

* * *

Sergei held himself in tight control. He knew what Leslie was feeling and thinking. He would not allow himself to impose his reactions and experiences on her. This time was crucial. He'd shared with her his descent into depression and in time spoke of his suicide attempts. She was the only person with whom he had been completely open. Like Leslie, Sergei had trained from three years old, reached the pinnacle of his career only to have it abruptly snatched away. He adored that she never judged anyone, including herself. She had an incomparable ability to step outside of herself and her own circumstances and analyze from a distance.

They'd been at his place on seventy-fifth street. Leslie swore he took the apartment because it was close to

Fairway, and not because it was in walking distance of Lincoln Center.

Fairway was supposed to be a market, but it was an institution. The produce was exceptional, the breads from all over Europe were exquisite and the cheeses and sausages were sublime. It was not unusual for them to have dark bread and cheese for dinner with a bottle of wine.

Now the season was over. They'd had dinner at their favorite Afro-Cuban restaurant. They sat on the floor with their backs against the sofa in front of the fireplace. They were at peace.

Sergei had opened a bottle of wine before they'd left, and now it was ready. He filled their glasses.

"Sergei, why did you attempt suicide? It was some time after you'd already changed everything."

"Loneliness. Retrospectively, it was the soul-breaking loneliness that I couldn't stand. It was okay when I was dancing and then while I was studying. It was the nights that got to me. I hadn't met you and I have always needed you in my life. Even during the rehab, I could manage. Pain can make you focus.

"Depression isn't an abstraction nor is it a choice. It is more complex than a chemical imbalance in the brain.

It is incapacitating, hence the number of suicides. It isn't understood and many reasons are given for its existence. I don't know if there is a cure yet."

He paused, "I believe I had been lonely all my life, but ballet was my friend and my confidant. My lover in a way. What I always felt on stage, in class or rehearsal was subliminal. It was not of this world. Even as a child of eight, I knew I was born to dance. In Russia when I grew up, that was an excellent thing. It would have been impossible for me to be trapped at a desk.

"I adore taking care of dancers. In an abstruse way, it is as satisfying as ballet. Different but the same. Does that make any sense?"

"I think so. Another expression of the same thing. A different medium or form of expression perhaps? I can feel your meaning."

"When I put someone back on the stage, I am exultant. Of course, it isn't just me. I must have a fighter, someone who is hungry and determined. Injuries are not just to the body; they are equally to the mind, and they batter the emotions. We live a life where the very thought of an injury can go beyond debilitating into incapacitation. It isn't just our bodies that are precarious. Our heads are just as vulnerable. Our emotions are on a permanent roller coaster ride.

"Les, it is like being an active mover in life. Sometimes I feel like I am part of nature when I breathe life back into a dancer. Bringing someone back to the stage is a feeling I cannot express in words. But I can tell you that it is the same feeling I had doing Don Quixote."

He was still for some time. Leslie was with him in that still place.

* * *

Leslie's mother Margaret had been a debutante and was now a dilettante. Margaret, who answered to Muffin, was a faded woman. Except for choosing which vodka to drink, she'd never been allowed to decide anything for herself. She found refuge in all things beautiful and took her two daughters to the opera, the ballet, and the theater. New York was a fast 58 minutes away from Chappaqua. Her husband Michael, like his father and grandfather, was an investment banker with JP Morgan. He was rarely at home, even on weekends. The gossip was that he couldn't bare the sight of his wife.

"Girls, figure out if you want a book or puzzles for the train and put them beside the door." The Metro North ride into New York was fun for the girls. They played games, talked to the other passengers or read their books. They went to every museum in New York and the various libraries.

They attended the opera, the theater and performances of all types of dance. Leslie's and Debra's exposure to the opulent culture of New York was complete.

When Leslie was three years old, she said she wanted to do what the ladies did on stage. "Mommy, I want to do that." They'd just seen a Swan Lake matinee.

Margaret said, "Leslie, ballet is very, very difficult. Those people practice for years and years and take classes every day. They make everything look graceful and easy."

"When can I start classes, I want to do that."

"You're very young."

"I want to take classes." Leslie yelled.

Since most ballet schools in Chappaqua only accepted students at five, it was some time before Margaret found a Russian school that would take her precocious three-year old. Though it was utterly irrelevant to Margaret, they explained that they specialized in the Vaganova Method.

The owner of the school was happy to discover that Leslie's little body was extraordinarily suited for ballet, strong, flexible and lithe. At a time when most young girls were plodding, Leslie was floating. The teachers at the school were surprised by her discipline and dedication at such an early age. By the time she was nine, her mother was

taking her to New York for ballet lessons five days a week and delighted to do it.

Debra played the piano and was gifted, and though Margaret encouraged her, she was not diligent. However, Leslie worked like one obsessed and it was clear that Leslie was a prodigy. She was accepted at the American Ballet Theater where she excelled. She was able to absorb elements of ballet like air. While still in her teens, she was invited to guest with several youth companies in Europe. She was a phenomenon written up in dance magazines and in major newspapers.

One local newspaper interviewed her and asked her about her gift. She was always surprised when people talked about her gift. All of it was very natural to her. Leslie said, "Of course, I never stop working my body because it is my tool. I learn all the steps, the music, and incorporate all the notes. Then, when I rehearse or when I am on stage, none of those things exists. Everything coalesces into a single breath that goes far beyond the pieces involved. Perhaps you could call it transcendent."

At twenty-seven, Leslie was living her dream. When she became the youngest principal in ABT's history, she invited everyone she knew to a champagne party at her apartment that her parents had given when she became a principal.

It was to be their last gift to her. During a freak storm, their helicopter went down in the Rockies. They never knew that her life had been shattered. They did know that she and her sister would each inherit massive fortunes.

At twenty-nine, her world dissolved. Doctors, chiros, and PTs said she would never dance again. Leslie was determined to prove every one of them wrong. Though he was a participant in help and support, Sergei said nothing. Leslie couldn't conceive of a life without dance.

She'd explored everything imaginable and put in the work. One day, Leslie finally understood. From then on, she'd put on her pointe shoes only for classes. The lights, the costumes, and the curtain calls would be for another prima ballerina.

After this realization she slept for three days, only arising to drink water and nibble on a little fruit and bread. Sergei came by to make sure she was all right. The third day when she awakened it was with a ravenous appetite and an inexplicable urge to travel.

Sergei had just arrived with fat blueberry muffins and croissants.

"Sergei, I must go abroad. Don't know why, I only know that I must."

Sergei was silent as he gathered her into his arms and kissed the top of her head.

"I imagine that something is waiting for you there. I am happy for this."

"Where should we go first? Russia, Scandinavia, North Africa, Europe?"

He held her away and looked into her deep dark eyes and said, "My love, you have healed. This is your rebirth. Yours alone. Your path must be of your own design, as it was to arrive where we are today. On the surface it may seem that things just happen, but that is never the case. Cause and effect rules the universe. It is in physics, in all the sciences really. You are full of talent and ability, and it hasn't ended. There is something happening for you."

Leslie was absorbing his words, "Then you're saying that my injury was not random or some coincidence, happenstance?"

"Yes. That is correct, though I have no idea of its meaning or direction. As you know, I speak from experience. You owe it to yourself to take these next steps on your own. Know that nothing is random."

"Is this why you haven't married me?"

"Probably. My sense has been that it hasn't been the right time for us. I've wanted to marry you since the instant we met. In fact, we are married and always will be."

Though disappointed, she did understand Sergei's intent and his rationale. She loved him with all her heart. He asked that they be old-fashioned and write letters to each other rather than make phone calls.

He said, "I believe that letters are more personal."

* * *

She rented a villa in the south of France just above Beaulieu and close to Nice. She spent time visiting castles, museums and walking the cobblestoned streets. That people still lived in buildings built four or five centuries ago fascinated Leslie. She booked classes to study French and hired a tutor to learn the history of the region. She absorbed an entirely different culture. She kept her distance from the tourists whom she found to be venal and, in many cases, obnoxious.

On the other hand, the locals had depth, were intelligent and content in life. They never ranted about being happy, yet it came through in everything they did. The young man who took care of the pool had a visit from his uncle. He introduced her and she discovered that he was a shepherd. After some conversation on their second encounter, she asked if she could spend a day shadowing him. She explained that she had never met a shepherd and did not know the true

meaning of the word or what the life of a shepherd really was. He liked her curiosity.

When they started out in the morning, Leslie was struck by how he communicated with the animals. He said that it was the same way that he communicated with people. His peace was ineffable. When they stopped for lunch on the hillside, the softness and meshing with the hills and the sky and the air took her breath away.

She became well known in the village shops. She garnered a reputation for being open and hungry for knowledge. She had help with the language and history everywhere she went. Much of the history was from individual experiences.

The food was wonderful. To be sure she did not poison herself, she hired a local chef. His lessons were invaluable. Some were in cooking. The main lessons were about living, truly living. Leslie had never heard anyone talk about cooking in the same way that she spoke of dance. In time, very gradually, she learned the art of cooking.

Sitting happily on her balcony one evening, looking out over Cap Ferrat, she felt something prodding her to go to Italy.

She'd planned to take the train to Venice, but at the last minute La Scala popped into her mind, and she booked a flight to Milan. Milan was dramatically different from her life in Villefranche. Milan was all things fashion, and it was

gorgeous. Leslie spent three days shopping for shoes, boots, bags, scarves, everything.

She called her friend, Chiara, who worked at La Scala, and got tickets for a performance. She was delighted to wear her new clothes and shoes. She settled into her seat and absorbed the luxury. The plush velvet seats, the gilt, the lights, design and ambiance were incomparable. When the lights went down, Leslie was ready for the experience.

As expected, the singing was magnificent, the conductor and orchestra were perfection. It was absolute heaven. When the ballet dancers came on stage, Leslie was almost jolted out of her seat. They were lifeless. They performed like mannequins in tutus. Leslie was aghast, insulted, and completely undone. The dancing, if it could be called that, was an abomination! Somehow, she made it through to the end of the opera and was gracious to her seatmates and left La Scala as a normal person. She was seething inside.

Leslie's name and accomplishments were still lauded throughout the dance world. Through Chiara, and with the proper introductions, she arranged to teach "master" classes for the dancers.

They did the requisite class of barre, center and finished with reverence. Then Leslie had the dancers sit on the floor with their eyes closed and listen to the music. They did this several times. Next, they stood in first position and followed

the music with their arms. Finally, they listened to the music with their bodies and imbibed the music. Each step took on a new life as the music and dancers became inseparable.

Leslie wanted to bring them to a new awareness, and inspiration. Her goal was to have each dancer draw out her own transcendence. Through experimenting and drawing on what she could see developing each day as she kept teaching, she learned how to imbue that illusive element into dancers. At the same time, there was the feeling that they already had it inside and that perhaps she was the vehicle to extract it. She did not know.

After ten days, they were unrecognizable as the same performers. They were alive, vibrant and stimulating.

She worked at La Scala as much as she could to refine her teaching technique. After two months, she was asked to coach at the Paris Opera. Her gift was alive and well and she could channel it into other people.

After two years abroad, it was time to go back to Sergei and back to New York.

In New York, Leslie walked incessantly, took classes, and envisioned a new way of life. There had always been students at the ABT who could not reach the audience as she did. She'd never thought about it. Collaborating with the dancers in Italy and France, she learned that there was

something almost magical within each dancer. She'd seen it. One dancer who was firmly entrenched in mediocrity had bloomed into magnificence. It was fantastic and soothed Leslie's soul.

Leslie learned that there were hidden talents and gifts in every person. She learned that she could unleash those hidden talents and gifts within people.

She presented her proposal to the ABT and, while there was skepticism, her reputation and achievements persuaded them to let her try this unprecedented undertaking at the school.

Leslie was overwhelmingly successful. To her, something subliminal occurred when the switch turned, or the light bulb went off in a dancer. The change was palpable; their dancing became distinctly different.

Soon she was in demand at other dance schools not only in New York but across the nation and in Europe. She wanted to expand beyond ballet though she had no idea where it would lead.

CHAPTER 2

AND THEN SHE COULD

Sophia Moretti did not want to go to work; she wanted to go to her dance class. But she'd have to wait until the evening.

Sophia at twenty-five, had indeed made something of herself. She was second-generation Italian. Her Neapolitan family had been farmers for generations. Mussolini and the war changed all that. And they fled. Her parents had arrived in the United States with guts, grit and little else.

Because they had been farmers, they understood life. Sophia grew up with an appreciation for life, with patience and a deep respect for nature. She could sit with herself and think without outside stimuli or entertainment. Farmers were not inclined to alter the reality of life. They don't attempt to rush the seasons, control nature or rush time.

Language was by no means the only obstacle in this new country.

Every night, they talked around the dinner table. Sometimes it was just Mama and Papa but a couple of times a week, friends from the neighborhood would stop in for coffee and talk. Sophia learned so much from the discussions and observations. Limited in English, Papa

worked in a factory and Mama in the garment district. They worked hard for their survival and for their beloved little Sophia. They'd lost two other children in the war.

Papa said, "I can't see why their talk is always about hate. I thought this was the land of opportunity. With so much opportunity why is there so much nasty talk about Jews, coloreds, and Puerto Ricans. Anybody who is not like them. They don't seem to like themselves. The country is enormous, with room for everyone. I can't understand why they try to horde things."

Mama chuckled and said, "At my shop, they are the worst on Mondays—after church on Sunday. When we went to church back home, people were calm and gentle. Here they seem to be raging and mean. Do you think it is just the times. The war was hideous for everyone."

"The churches here are different. They don't resemble our Roman Catholic ones at home. And the people are rude and condescending. Why is everything lip service?" said Papa.

"I'm not going anymore; I have had enough hypocrisy. So many people seem to live without any foundation in their lives. Have you noticed that the focus is on things and not people or goodness. They just float, follow, and fade. And the priests are strange too."

Papa sighed, "I agree. They are unstable and easily frightened."

"Lots of lunatics," Mama said. "Yesterday one of the girls was talking about instant coffee. Well, she brought some in for us to taste. It was ghastly, absolute swill! She was raving about it because it took no time to make. I asked her if she liked the taste and she said it didn't matter because it was so easy to make. Ugh."

The attitudes they encountered often made things inconvenient, at the same time it was another form of education. Sophia and her family learned how to incorporate the positive while ignoring behavior which could only be identified as madness.

When Sophia was nineteen, Mama had a heart attack and died. Though Papa ranted and ranted, Sophia dropped out of college.

"Sophia, I don't want you to work like Mama and me. You are smart and talented, you need college."

"And you need support," said Sophia. "We can't make it on one salary."

She took a job with the electric company. She excelled and moved up the ladder until she was a manager, one of the first female managers. She had heard every snide comment about being a woman, a wop and anything else they could

drum up. Sophia kept her eyes on her goal. It was amusing how frustrated her detractors became when they couldn't rattle her. She applied for a job at an advertising firm that offered full tuition reimbursement for college. She was on her way, except that she wasn't.

Her father told her not to leave the electric company, "They have been so good to you, and every year you get a nice raise. It isn't like a pizzeria, or a factory job which is always the same. You are lucky. Don't tempt fate."

Her father had virtually died when Mama did. He'd become tentative, unsure of himself and unsure of life. He was a shadow of the man he had once been. "Sophia, Sophia you are a very good girl. I want you to get married and settle down."

"Papa, something is missing, and I don't really know what it is. Making money isn't enough. Making it in America isn't enough. Moving up isn't enough. I do not know what I want or need. I just have to keep looking for it." She gave her father a long hug. She knew that he understood.

Like many immigrants, disillusionment with the dream had happened quickly. The promise of opportunity was not as it was portrayed. It was an opportunity for people already here to prey upon newcomers. So much meanness. As she grew older and analyzed it, she felt it was because immigrants

were confronted with a wall of greed, anger and ignorance. She never found the brotherly love she had heard about.

Singing was in her Italian blood, yet oddly, Sophia felt a much deeper connection to dance.

She went to Steps On Broadway for her first class which was Beginning Tap. Because of fear, it had taken several months for her to enroll in the class. When she finally did, she paid for a package so that she would not make excuses and quit. Steps was impressive for its teachers, the ambiance and the effectiveness of the instruction. Daytime sessions were full of professional dancers from the theater or ballet companies. In the evening, though the bricks and paint remained the same, it was a different place. Mail carriers, secretaries, lawyers, doctors, messengers all put on tights, character shoes, tap shoes, or ballet shoes and danced into their dreams.

Sophia wanted to do this but still when she entered her first class, her eyes were wild with terror. It took a months of taking classes twice a week before her hands stopped shaking uncontrollably when she danced. Her teacher, a former Broadway dancer, was kind and encouraging. He told her to stop looking down at the floor and to look at herself in the mirror. Sophia was shocked at the difference that made. It was a new universe. She took dance classes after work and dropped out of college. She went to every

conceivable class she could and reveled in the freedom that came with it.

Her co-worker, Stephanie suggested a new class she'd found that was very unusual. That was enough to intrigue Sophia. They arrived early and watched the end of the class before. It was taught by a small woman; she was average height and slender but there was something different. Somehow, their eyes connected. The instructor's eyes were gentle and knowing. Sophia sensed something timeless. She stayed and had the most transcendent experience ever. The teacher's name was Leslie.

The way she moved was like nothing Sophia had ever seen before. It was mesmerizing because it was coordinated, smooth and powerful at the same time. She said to the class that anyone could move as she did. Sophia believed her. The beginning and intermediate classes, there was intense ballet work and included Pilates and stretching. In the more advanced classes, the music was from every imaginable genre. It could be jazz, salsa, ballet, soft-shoe, theater, African or Middle Eastern. She said it was all the same language and if the body were supple, the music was just the guide.

In three years, Sophia did move the way that Leslie did. People often asked her if she were a dancer. At first, she was startled and laughed outright. Then she began to appreciate

what was really a miracle of sorts. She'd become incredibly strong and flexible. There was fluidity in her movements. Sophia had entered the world of dance in one form and had allowed the dance to alter her. It was beyond physical and her outlook on life had undergone a sea-change.

One evening after an especially difficult class, Leslie asked to chat with Sophia after she had changed. When she came out, Leslie held an issue of Backstage and showed Sophia an upcoming audition for a Broadway show.

"Sophia, you could nail this."

Sophia said nothing. She could only stare at the page, then at Leslie and then back at the page again. She felt as though she were in rushing water with thunder and lightning all around her.

Leslie was suggesting that Sophia pursue her secret, unspoken dream.

* * *

Sophia adored everything about the theater. She'd started going to matinees with Mama as a little girl. They'd take the subway from Brooklyn. Usually, they'd have a potato knish because they both adored them. Mama liked shows with lots of singing, for Sophia, it was the dancing. When she started working, she spent more money on shows

than on clothes and makeup. A Chorus Line, Chicago, The Wiz, 42nd Street, Cats, Sophia had seen them all as many times as she could. These shows kindled something within her that she could not explain. It was later that she spent most of her money on dance classes, shoes, and dancewear.

Sophia studied New York theater history and was surprised to learn that Broadway had such a long history. She studied the lives of performers on Broadway and of those on the big screen. She loved the big dance movies with Fred Astaire, the Nicholas Brothers and James Cagney. Initially, she couldn't accept that singing and dancing was work or could be called a job. To Sophia, it seemed like heaven and the greatest fun imaginable.

Sophia had no one she could talk to about her feelings and thoughts. Her friends were also children of immigrants and among them there was no room for ideas that didn't bring in money or offer an opportunity to move up.

She had been hardwired to achieve the American Dream.

Deep in her heart, she knew she didn't want it.

CHAPTER 3
AND HE WAS CALLED

One summer evening, Alvaro noticed a woman in the crowd who was totally focused and intense. She stayed and stayed which wasn't so unusual because people often did. But there was an aura about her. Finally, she put money in his pot and a note.

At a break, she approached him and asked him if they could meet to talk about dance.

* * *

Sullivan & Cromwell was one of the oldest and most prestigious New York law firms. The firm was exacting, demanding precision in every aspect and in every department in the firm. Its round-the-clock copy center was always busy and had to provide documents for deals involving many millions of dollars. Errors were costly for the firm; they were even more costly for the employee who made them.

By day Alvaro Perez was manager of S&C's bustling copy center in the heart of the financial district. At night he was a highly skilled street performer near Lincoln Center.

One of six children, Alvaro had done odd jobs since he was ten. He was smart and ambitious, but his greatest asset

was curiosity. He always went one step beyond what was required. Even as a toddler, he had kept his little space in order. Law firms demanded specificity and order; Alvaro excelled at both. Some of the partners at Sullivan and Cromwell knew who he was because he had saved the day on more than one occasion.

Alvaro asked innumerable questions when repair people came and then got books from the library and taught himself to repair the machines. He constantly researched the latest in copiers so that they had the most up-to-date, efficient and reliable copiers available. After five years with the firm, they took his suggestions without question. They had also suggested that he consider going to law school. They were prepared to pay for it.

Alvaro always sensed when something was out of kilter or even slightly "off" which was a terrific advantage when he performed. He was sure it had prevented injuries and other incidents. He always knew that there was another dimension to which he had no access. He wanted access to it.

New Yorkers are a tough crowd. Discerning, strict and demanding, they would go out of their way to show appreciation, yelling for encore after encore and tossing more tens, twenties and fifties into the pot. With that same energy they would cheerfully pan anyone who dared to

perform and couldn't cut it. Good street performers earned well. He did this for some time on his own, always around Columbus Circle, then began to work with others who were at his skill level. Having someone steal the pot after a rigorous performance was the ultimate low.

Born in the Bronx of Puerto Rican and Cuban parents, he grew up in a vibrant culture, with great food, music, dance, and vivacity. Young boys used to compete by out-singing or out-dancing one another. And everybody was catholic. He loved the order of church music and the sound of the organ.

The day he saw Mikhail Baryshnikov on television changed his life. Not only did Alvaro want to know how Baryshnikov did what he did, he wanted to do it too. Alvaro envisioned Baryshnikov when he choreographed his routines.

He went to the library to learn more about ballet and more about Baryshnikov. He borrowed books on ballet. He scoured the newspapers for news of when and where he could see his idol perform in New York.

At fifteen, he'd quietly begun taking ballet lessons at Steps. He felt he was drawing closer to that dimension he knew existed. He had never felt so fulfilled in his entire life. He loved the barre, the plies and the tendues. Doing

the center was mind-blowing. The combinations were extraordinary, and he was high whenever he left class.

Naturally, the discipline, strengthening and exactitude of ballet drastically altered his performances.

He thought about this lady and wondered what she wanted.

* * *

Most people envied him. It was a terrific firm, beautiful, well-run and organized. He loved the work, the people, and daily challenges. Alvaro also felt trapped.

He needed to make a decision. At twenty-four, the offer of a free ride for law school was thought-provoking. He liked the symmetry of law and believed that the work would be stimulating and sometimes elating. And the income wouldn't be too shabby. He knew he could ace it through law school because he would work to accomplish it. The partners knew that. And they knew he was smart.

Still, it didn't feel right.

* * *

Alvaro knew he had a talent. He did not know what to do with it except to constantly get better. He loved moving people with his performances. To him performing was a

form of communication. There was something magical that happened when he performed. Though he knew it was there, he had never been able to express it properly. He thought it was in that other dimension that he had yet to touch.

Alvaro also knew that he had to pay bills and help his family and relatives. He'd done the math a few years ago to see if he could support everyone with just street performances. It was possible. At the same time there was no health insurance and there were no sick days. There were snow days, hurricanes and during the summers, the temperatures were in the hundreds.

He wished that there were a way to dance, be paid for it, and support his family. But that was not how the system worked.

One of his uncles had been encouraging him to allow his family to take more responsibility. His father was a drinker and his mother had given up on life, while his siblings had jobs, they were not aggressive or interested in advancing in their lives. His uncle pointed out that they had no need because they had a resident bank called Alvaro. They borrowed a lot of money from him. He had been the financial pillar of the family since he was fifteen. He had grown weary of this and knew that they did not need to rely on him. It was merely a habit.

If he proceeded to go to college and law school; he would be the first of his relatives to do so.

He told no one in his family about the offer.

* * *

Sergei had almost crushed her when they met at the airport. Leslie thought it was the best thing ever.

They were at her place. He'd had it cleaned, aired and had fresh flowers delivered.

Sergei said, "I have a gift for you."

"Really? You are gift enough."

He presented a bound album with all the letters she had written to him.

Sergei said, "Your letters are an odyssey. Through them you detailed your new awareness, new language, new people. I felt as though I were there."

Leslie stroked the velvet cover, "This is perfect. Thank you."

The tears started to trickle and quickly turned into a deluge. Sergei held her and happily let her drench his shirt. She cried for a long time.

Finally, he dried her face and said, "I have reservations at your favorite restaurant. We have four hours...."

Later, when they were seated at a lovely table with a view of the park sipping their port, She said, "Sergei, you knew before I left what would happen. I felt you everywhere I went. It was wonderful."

"Not exactly, I sensed 'something' was about to happen that was life-changing which would go far beyond the injury."

She nodded. "It is almost impossible to express. Too many people with immense talent have been put on automatic doing nine-to-five. My time in France showed that it doesn't have to be music, dance or opera. Gifts manifest in many ways.

"Right now, I think we can do something about the dancers. If we focus, then we will be able to change many lives. Perhaps we can free nine-to-fivers who want to do something different."

"Any ideas about how we can do this?"

"Let's go back home and break it down."

At home, they brought out a white board, plenty of paper, markers and put on the coffee.

Sergei said, "The first thing is our main idea. We want to support anyone who has a dream to become a performer. Right now, that should be in dance because I know you can't sing."

He ducked as an eraser sailed by his head. "What will it look like?"

"Should it be a school for younger people or an after work program for those who are older?"

"We both started at three, but Nureyev didn't. I know there are more people like Nureyev who are typing, doing word processing or writing briefs."

"What's the best approach?"

"Sergei, I forgot to tell you. Debra wants to be part of this."

"Great. What has she been doing?"

"She has been being bored. Little excites her and nothing has inspired her to drive herself. She is happy about what we are doing and wants to help. She lives in the house in Chappaqua and putters around in the garden. She is considering writing a book about gold-diggers."

Sergei laughed and said, "Debra is so capable. Once we have the dance organized maybe she could do something on the musical end."

"Good idea."

Leslie was chewing on a pencil. "I think we should start off gradually. I have seen people from different schools and

classes I believe would be good prospects for this. There are two I would like you to meet very soon."

"Sounds good," he said, "having a concrete idea is key. With a solid foundation, we can start building. Right now, we don't even what we are doing."

"We may not know what we are doing, but we know this is right. As painful and shattering as everything has been, I know that what has come of it is vital." She kissed him.

"That is exactly how I feel about my work."

They settled into a comfortable silence.

CHAPTER 4

AWAKENING

On her many walks around the city, Leslie learned lessons in life. She looked at everything with a different eye. She wondered what gifts the young man delivering packages might have. At the coffee shop, she wondered about the server. She wondered about the secretaries, postal workers, doctors and lawyers.

Because she often went to restaurants and shops during off hours, people had more time to have conversation. The number of dreams and goals were astounding.

She was certain that most people had jobs that didn't match their talent or abilities. Her cooking classes in France had opened her in a myriad of ways. She knew that most things were not what they seemed. Job offerings were one-dimensional. In fact, there were very few options for most people. She began to question why certain choices were made.

From a far different vantage point, she learned that most jobs were down to basic survival. People would take any job to provide food and shelter for their families. Given a choice between pursuing their own dreams, they would always opt to provide. The world did not allow an outlet

for artistic expression. This world was based on the idea that one should work and ignore anything that did not generate money.

This was the issue that most disturbed Leslie.

Until her injury, she'd never thought about money, or that it could be an obstacle to pursuing a goal. She learned that for many it was an absolute block. There was no doubt that there were many who had talent equal her own.

She knew she couldn't change everything, but her goal was to give as many people as possible the opportunity to maximize their dreams.

She learned that many workers lived for the weekend when they did not have to go to work. In many instances, people loathed their jobs, but could not do without them.

They awakened to a brilliant fall day in New York. Sergei opened the drapes to a magnificent view of the park. Riverside Drive was awash in fall colors.

He paused and looked out of window and said, "This is the most gorgeous area of the City. It's quiet and not commercial and I always feel like the park is our backyard. How did your parents find this gem?"

Leslie came in and put her arms around his waist and enjoyed the view. "This and several other buildings were

investments. The buildings from seventy-second to ninety-sixth have stunning architecture and the curves and hills along the drive were carefully designed. When property values dropped, Father's group or company bought a bunch. This building was his favorite. So, it belongs to us. I hadn't even considered it, maybe there is potential."

Leslie ground the beans for coffee. Both were coffee-lovers, and they had the beans shipped from Colombia once a month. The aroma of the beans alone was enough to send any coffee connoisseur into ecstasy.

Sergei was putting together a breakfast fruit salad. With a sly grin he said, "I have a surprise for later."

"You've been to Fairway again, I know it!"

In the alcove with a bay window, they ate in silence until their second cup.

"Luv, maybe I am on to something. Let's settle on what the goal is. Is it superstardom, money, fame, an opportunity to perform once or twice a week? We can't create anything without a solid goal in mind. If we know where we are headed, finding the road is easy."

"You're right," she said. "For me it was always the joy of dancing and I never thought about any of those things. What about you?"

"It was the same," he said. "Maybe I am going out on a limb, but too much focus is on money. When was the last time you heard about anybody talking about joy or happiness? That is what I hear coming through when I listen to the back stories on American Idol and shows like it. Each one of the participants has a full time job. And their lives are screaming for something more than that daily grind. Make no mistake, I imagine it works for some people.

"But it doesn't work for someone whose gift is howling to get out. It cannot. So, the question goes back to how can we create a vehicle that allows that expression and provides a sustainable income for these artists?"

"A production isn't the answer because it's too short-lived. Broadway shows aren't a vehicle for long-term work. Television and cable shows rarely last long."

"Too many people consider the arts to be 'lower than,' hobbies, silly, or not 'real' work. I would love to have some of these people in class just for thirty minutes. They have no imagination." Sergei smiled with relish.

"And they never will have. We don't need to change their minds. We need to create a vehicle for these immensely talented artists."

He said, "Maybe we're looking at this the wrong way round."

"What do you mean."

"Why don't you continue doing what you have been doing? You have already begun crafting a new tapestry for some artists whom you have met. We need that degree change that will create a profitable career."

"Jobs today are killing people because many are doing jobs they do not like, to make money to impress people they don't like. This is stressful and the number of heart attacks on Monday morning is telling.

"The other piece that baffles me is that if someone makes money, he or she is respected. If an individual makes huge profits at the expense of people's lives or health, that is immaterial. It makes me shudder. How can anyone blithely shop at Prada, when the money with which they are shopping comes from child labor or other sorts of obscenity?"

"Of course, you are right," she said. "Rhetorical question—Why doesn't anyone know or care about these things?"

"I read that people have been indoctrinated to such an extent that they are immune to horrors perpetrated upon other people. I don't believe they have the capacity to analyze what is happening around them or to them. Unfortunately, there's no guarantee that it would make any difference to them."

"What exactly do you mean about continuing?"

"You said there are two people you want me to meet, and you have mentioned things about them from time to time. What are your plans for them? How will you expose their gift to the universe?"

"I see where you are going with this and I like it," she said. "Sophia looks like she has been dancing since she was born. She moves like a panther, smooth, agile and powerful. Sergei, she took her first dance class when she was in her early twenties. Her talent and abilities have always been inside of her.

"I suggested she do a Broadway audition. She did and she got the role. She is devastated because she has a full time job with security. It is a valid quandary because Broadway isn't known for longevity nor stability.

"My other gifted performer is Alvaro. I did not know what to make of him the first time I saw him perform. He is a break dancer with dash. I saw a lot of ballet technique combined with natural talent. Like Sophia, he has a responsible job with all the bells and whistles."

"Les, we have to find the solution."

CHAPTER 5
LEGACY

Sophia decided that she hated Leslie. It was all Leslie's fault that she was in this awful predicament.

Leslie had somehow read her mind and suggested that audition. It was truly wonderful to do. Sophia couldn't understand why the other dancers were so sloppy in their movements. Well, they weren't sloppy, just sloppy from Sophia's point of view.

She would never have thought of going on the audition or any other for that matter. She'd automatically assumed that the other dancers would be light years beyond her. That was not the case.

The audition process took two days. It was intense, grueling and downright brutal, yet Sophia was never overwhelmed, frightened, or insecure. That was because of the training she had received.

She got the job.

And that was why she hated Leslie.

Now she didn't know what to do. She was sure about one thing. She could never tell her father. It would put him in his grave.

She couldn't just quit. She'd have to take a leave of absence. And what about her health insurance, vacations, her 401K. This had no guarantees, though in truth, nothing really had any guarantees.

What was she going to do?

Leslie was home alone thinking through their mission. Sergei was at the ABT taking care of the dancers. She couldn't wait until he returned.

She thought that they should meet with Sophia and Alvaro. She suspected that Sophia and Alvaro would thrive together. She and Sergei couldn't make decisions for them without their input. There was no doubt that they would understand what they were trying to do.

She called Sergei and he agreed, so she called her proteges. They were both intrigued although she couldn't understand why Sophia said she was going to kill her.

He met Leslie at a cafe near Lincoln Center. He was surprised to discover that he liked her immediately. He felt that she was part of that other dimension he had never reached.

"Thank you for taking the time to meet me, Alvaro," she said.

"No problem. I am always curious about anything to do with dance."

"From the way you dance, perhaps you follow the ballet. I am Leslie Beaumont, and I was a prima ballerina with the American Ballet Theater until an injury stopped my career."

"I think I have heard of you. I am sorry to hear about your injury," said Alvaro. "Yes, I am sure of it. I have seen you dance at Lincoln Center. Without a tutu, pointe shoes, and makeup, I didn't recognize you. Sorry."

She laughed. "Believe me, no one recognizes us offstage. For one thing, we have clothes on."

He liked her even more. She had a twinkle in her eye and certainly wasn't someone interested in lamenting the loss of a brilliant career.

She asked, "You are ballet-trained, aren't you?"

"Well, yes. I started when I was fifteen. I saw Baryshnikov and was hooked. He is magnificent and I wanted to do that. My teacher said my body is perfect for ballet. I asked him what that meant, and he said I had natural turnout, feet, extreme flexibility and was strong."

"I know exactly what he meant, and I couldn't agree more. The reason I asked to meet you is because of your extreme talent...."

"Extreme talent?" He blurted.

"Oh definitely. I see it every day, and it is easy to recognize. It is also exceedingly rare. When I stopped dancing, I did

about fourteen months rehab and then I traveled. I made a remarkable discovery. It was really a twofold discovery."

"I am intrigued."

"The first is that many professional dancers have no idea how to draw out the depths of their talent. I had never thought about anything like that. Like you, for me it was just a natural thing. When I was abroad, I learned that it was possible to develop that in any dancer. Too many dancers perform without delving deeply into their souls. Their dancing would bore you to tears. Awful."

"I never heard anyone say it that way. I see what you mean. What is the second thing?"

"That is trickier to explain," she said. "Sergei and I talk about this all the time. Do you know Sergei Orlov? He was with the Kirov and then with the ABT."

"Of course, I know him. He is like Baryshnikov, only younger. He is great. Wasn't he injured?"

"Yes, he was. We make quite the couple," Leslie said laughing again.

"We agree that it isn't just people who trained from a very early age, who are gifted. As with you and another new friend, the gift is there. 'When ya got it, ya got it.' As the saying goes."

"It isn't just with dance. It is with voice, with art, with music and with so many things where people are enormously talented, and that talent is left untapped. We are trying to find a way be a conduit to unleash those gifts. We don't know how yet and that is why I wanted to speak with you."

"Leslie, I have always felt that there is another dimension, if that is the right word. These ideas and perceptions belong in that dimension. I wish there were a way to be paid to do what I do at night. It is thrilling, challenging and I never tire of it. Pushing my body, finding new pinnacles is what I live for. At least, at night. I work for a law firm in the day."

"Yes, I can appreciate that. It could be that we are here to pull those talents from others. Maybe making people aware of their gifts is the answer. I don't know. Not yet."

Alvaro thought that it was no coincidence that he was having this discussion.

He said, "I don't believe in coincidences."

"Nor do I."

CHAPTER 6
REALIZATION

Sophia was ambivalent about Leslie's suggestion to meet. On the one hand, it would give her an opportunity to murder her. And on the other she was curious.

They met at the Oyster Bar in Grand Central Station. The clam chowder was the best in New York.

Leslie was waiting for her. "Thank you for meeting me, Sophia. I appreciate it," she said. "But tell me why you have become homicidal."

Sophia burst into tears and sobbed for a long time. Leslie was taken aback and could only offer tissues and soothing noises. She had no idea what was wrong.

After some time, Sophia calmed down and said, "Leslie, I got it."

"Got what?"

"Oh, sorry. I got the show. Two days of non-stop dancing, testing and picking up and playing at being a swing. The worst thing they did was say we'd do the combination three times. First to make sure of the steps, second for practice and the third was to go full out and we'd be judged on that. There was no third time. They were looking for people who never marked, people who always gave their all. I got it."

When it looked like another bout of hot tears, Leslie quickly jumped in, "I'll order prosecco to celebrate." As she tried to signal a server.

"No, no, no," Sophia sobbed. "I can't do it; I have a job and responsibilities. My job is secure and, and, and . . ."

Leslie said, "I see. You want to do the show. You haven't declined then?"

"How on earth could I turn it down after dancing my feet off for two days. My feet are still sore."

"When do rehearsals start?"

"In two weeks."

"Let's make some plans," she said. "First, apply for a leave of absence at your job. Then you must tell your father. I suspect that he will be less devastated than you think. He is from the old country and is resilient. Next, get all the gear you need for rehearsals right away. The first few days or weeks you'll be half dead from the rehearsals. Make sure to pay attention to your notes."

"Just let me kill you. This is all your fault. Why did you suggest I do the audition? Do you know how many people showed up? It was unbelievable."

"And they chose you out of all those people. Seems to me it's your fault for being so talented."

"ARRGGHH%(*&&%%^!!!," growled Sophia.

"I see we're on the same page now."

"What did you want to talk about?"

Leslie said, "It is interesting that by winning that audition, against all odds, you proved exactly what Sergei and I believe.

"We feel that there are so many people who have exquisite talent and abilities in all forms of art. Most of them are doing the nine-to-five gig, by default. I don't think everyone wants to be in an office exchanging hours for dollars. It does work for some. However, many are dissatisfied with what they are doing but they see no recourse."

Sophia nodded and said, "That just about describes me."

"Aha, but you just proved the point. If you had not gone on that audition, how would you feel in two months, or two years, or twenty years? If you had not started classes some years ago, would you be as vibrant and alive as you are today? Even with your homicidal tendencies.

"You just cried your eyes out at the thought of rocking the boat. You are not alone. You just happen to be braver than the average person. Much braver."

"After all these years, I couldn't turn this down. I am terrified because I don't know where this will lead, or what could happen. It is as though I am walking on air."

"You will have your Equity Card."

"It is funny that you said there are so many people with dreams and talent. When I was going to evening classes, I loved to listen to the dreams and ideas of the other students. The wealth of ideas is amazing. I may be one of a few who will have the opportunity to live my dream even a tiny bit."

"It was definitely talent. But you can never overlook working extremely hard. And you put in the work. The secret to genius is work. Never forget that. There are a lot of people with genius, enormous talent and magnificent ideas, but it is just potential. Potential is potential until the arduous work starts—and never stops."

"Can I hug you?" They hugged.

"Leslie, I have never been this frightened in my life, even when my mother died."

"I know Sophia. I know. You will thrive and be a shining light on Broadway."

* * *

Leslie was cutting the black bread and shaving cheese for dinner when Sergei arrived.

"How was your day? Anything new?"

"My day was wonderful because I learned so much. Do you remember I told you about Sophia? She's the one

I suggested take an audition. There must have been just under two hundred at the call. She got it. It is kind of funny now, but she was crying her eyes out because she got the audition, couldn't turn it down, and now has to leave her shell forever."

Sergei sat down. "Didn't she start dancing at twenty?"

"Yep."

"That is mind-blowing. There is so much in what we are attempting to do. You have people like Sophia and Alvaro. And then people like the ones at La Scala. Opposite ends of the pole, but the essence is the same. Sleeping talent."

He started prepping the salad. "We have our work cut out for us."

* * *

They had the meeting at Leslie's place.

By 10:00 Saturday morning, everyone was comfortable with coffee and a pastry reading notes. Every now and then someone would add to the white board.

All agreed that there had to find a way to loosen peoples restraints. Some were real and as Alvaro and Sophia were experiencing some were due to brainwashing. They went over the ideas, details, possibilities, and liabilities. They played the devil's advocate with each other. Frustration was the fifth person in the room.

Alvaro said, "Let's do an analysis. Use my situation. I am responsible for my family. Would it be wise or rational to go full time into street performance?"

Sophia added, "I am in the same situation. I just got a show which should run for six to eight months. I am delighted but also fearful."

"What if you both do what I do?" said Leslie, "Sophia, you told me about the dreams of office workers you heard in the changing rooms. Alvaro, how did you meet the other street performers that you work with?"

Leslie saw light dawning on their faces.

"Got it." Alvaro said. "But this is only one piece of the puzzle."

Sergei offered, "I agree with you. We must keep brainstorming. There is a way to do this, but it is hidden."

Sergei looked at the clock, "It's almost 2:00 anybody up for lunch?"

"I should get some shopping done, and I need to talk with Papa," Sophia said looking at Leslie.

Alvaro looked rather disappointed but recovered quickly. "I'll walk you to the train."

"Great. Thanks," Sophia said.

Everyone said their goodbyes. And the young people left.

Giggling, Leslie and Sergei ran to the window to watch them. As they walked down the street, their body language said that they were at ease with each other.

"Do you think love is in the air?" asked Sergei.

"No question."

"Yup. We can start planning their wedding present."

"Come on, so soon?"

"Absolutely, Alvaro had his mind made up the minute he saw her."

"Really?"

"Alvaro knows his own mind. He is discerning and well balanced. He knows what he wants. He's probably known for a long time. He won't play around. He is definite."

"Hmmm, maybe I should add matchmaking to my repertoire."

"Well, you nailed these two."

* * *

Alvaro thought Sophia was the loveliest woman he had ever met. And so feminine. He loved women who were feminine, he thought femininity was the most wonderful thing in the world. Her elegance showed in the way she dressed. She was intelligent and really thought about life carefully. She also happened to be extremely pretty.

Sophia loved that Alvaro was so vibrant. He reminded her of her uncles. He was very responsible and cared about his family. She loved that he was stable and had a solid foundation in his life. On a scale of one to ten, he was a solid sixteen.

"When will rehearsals begin?"

"In roughly two weeks."

"May I take you out to dinner every night until you start?"

Sophia laughed and laughed until tears started, and her side was aching. She had to stop walking. "Alvaro, I love your honesty. I have never met anyone like you before. I am so happy to know you."

"I am very happy to know you as well. I want to know

everything about you."

* * *

The pigeons were watching them, their necks moving in that funny way. The one with the blue fleck said, "This is a fine couple. Usually, the fellow won't say what he feels and the girl acts like a mummy. What is left is confusion and misunderstanding. It is all very silly. I wonder why they do that."

The one with the red fleck said, "Yes, these two are wonderful. They are sensible. They'll be married before the year is out."

Someone tossed some bread and without ado, the two darted after it.

* * *

Alvaro asked, "How did you start dancing."

"Alvaro, I fell in love with Broadway. My mother used to take me to the matinees on Saturday, and I became enchanted. Tap was my first love until Leslie happened. What about you?"

"Baryshnikov. Baryshnikov made me a ballet addict. I saw him on television and couldn't believe his jumps and how easy they were. Well, how easy he made them look. He is so precise that I consider him a work of art. I started

ballet at Steps when I was fifteen and haven't ever stopped. It is uncanny that you and I never met at Steps."

"Probably because we were supposed to meet now."

"I agree. I am so glad we are finally together. I know you haven't too much time. Do you think you have time for a coffee or a glass of wine?"

"Yes, a quick one."

All Alvaro wanted to do was to kiss Sophia. Her lips looked so soft. She was lovely.

Sophia was swept away. She knew she would marry Alvaro. Right now, she wanted to hug him for about an hour.

"Will this café do?" Alvaro asked.

She said, "Oh yes. Thank you." She noticed not one thing.

Somehow, they were in each other's arms. And when he kissed her, time stood still. That is, until pedestrians started whistling and clapping. New Yorkers are hopeless romantics.

CHAPTER 7
THESIS

Leslie was in her wonderful bath. She loved baths and had hers customized. Water jets came from different directions and there was a rain shower as well. The floor and towel rods were heated. She could lie back, relax and think in her very own special place.

For the first time, Leslie had begun to read about New York and its history. She had not liked, nor had she enjoyed learning about the factories, sweatshops and other unsavory things. What was clear to her was that much of the unhappiness that people caused each other was unnecessary. She could not right it all, but she was determined to make a change in the arts, at least.

Both she and Debra knew about their parents' philanthropy, yet she had never thought beyond that. She did not want to toss money at a cause or make donations, she wanted to make changes. For her it was visceral.

Sergei had always talked about cause and effect. She had listened and agreed but she had not fully understood the depth of what he was saying. She was beginning to do so now, and it was exhilarating.

In her wonderfully warm bath, Leslie started to consider the swirls and eddies that make up the complexities of the world. She thought that if more people considered the repercussions of their actions, it would make them think more carefully about what they did.

Leslie thought this was too simplistic, but maybe not. It was just physics. Whenever one object exerts a force on a second object, the second object exerts an equal and opposite force on the first. It was something she had read about Newton. His third law is that for every action or force, there is an equal and opposite reaction.

She thought it made sense. She considered that if she could made only positive causes for a certain period, there would be positive results.

She wanted to make it possible for people to pursue and achieve their dreams. This world dictates that they never dreams and live like automatons.

The nine to five grind, living for the weekend, and having no dreams.

She thought this wasn't such a wonderful way to live.

* * *

Sergei and Leslie took a hamper and a blanket and walked to Central Park. As soon as they entered the park, the sounds

of the city were gone. There was an instant quiet and they felt as though they had entered another dreamlike realm.

It was a perfect backdrop for them to make their plans.

They spread the blanket and settled down and looked at each other and burst into laughter. It went on for some time until tears were rolling down their faces.

"Leslie, what are we doing?"

"Do you think I have any idea!! We know we are right, and we know what we want. The fact that we have no clue of how to do it is just a minor detail."

"Are we mad to even attempt any of this?"

"Of course, we are mad. That's a foregone conclusion. So, we just have to get on with it."

Sergei drew out their notes and started to review them. Leslie took a fresh pad and began to write.

Something obvious was missing. Something to do with La Scala, Sophia, and Alvaro. Some connection. She started pacing. Then she ran back to their blanket.

"Sergei, I think this is it!"

"What is it luv?"

"Let's do something that is a school for training, something like American Idol on a smaller scale, and a

touring company. The touring company could be for teens, or younger. Think the Mickey Mouse Club in a new way. They would get the training, grooming and experience. Many people find their gifts are in the background like choreographing, lighting, staging, or costuming."

Sergei said nothing. Just stared. Silence.

He looked at her without seeing, his mind was racing. "Yes, that is it! It's perfect and has everything we want. A place to train, a way to perform and share gifts. You are a genius."

"There are so many studios, but do you think we should have our own designated building or space?"

"We should definitely have our own place. Let's decide on its location. It'll need to be large. The first floor will be a performance venue, maybe a restaurant. That would be a bonus for those hidden chefs."

Leslie said, "I'll call Daddy's company about finding and buying a building. It should be in the fifties on the West Side. They can take our specifications and when they locate a few suitable buildings, we can look. The company is wonderful, and the same people have been there for ages. I think they will like our project and be very helpful. They'll also know the best builders and construction companies."

"I'll start trawling for ballet, tap, theater and gymnastics teachers. There are plenty of great teachers, but I will only work with the ones who can commit to our vision. It's a good thing I was consulted when we refurbished the ABT studios two years ago. I have all the information on the floors, barres and mirrors."

Leslie's eyes were glistening as she said, "Once we have the building, we can gauge the time we'll need for the renovation. In the meantime, we can create our outline for classes and our menu."

Something was welling inside of Sergei. It was time.

He dropped to one knee and said, "Leslie, you are the love of my life. You are my very life. Will you marry me?"

She never answered, she just fell into his arms and stayed there. She kept saying, "I love you; I love you." Repeatedly.

That was the end of their work for the day.

* * *

Leslie called Debra at 6:00 am the next morning.

"Debra, we're getting married!"

"I am so happy for you both. I can feel how perfect it is for you at this time. You both had your own careers and now you have a career together. Perfect."

She yawned and said, "When is the wedding? Will it be big or small?"

"Oh, I hadn't thought about that." Leslie stopped for a moment.

"I think it should be tiny," she said. "I will check with Sergei, but my sense is that it should be really small. And very soon."

"What'll you wear?"

"A forties style suit, maybe Versace or Prada. A hat gloves. Very forties. Jimmy Choo shoes."

"Sounds like a vision." Yawning again, Debra continued, "I have been talking about our project and lots of my friends on the various boards think it is fascinating. Someone suggesting finding an angel and one suggested being one. We will have lots of funding and support in other ways as well. I am going back to sleep, goodbye." And hung up.

* * *

Three days later, Mr. Farrell from the company phoned to say they'd found a jewel of a place on West 57th Street and Tenth Avenue. It was an enormous, abandoned warehouse which was structurally sound and had six floors.

When they arrived, Sergei and Leslie were astounded. They thought a genie had conjured up the perfect location

and details. It was on the corner and two entrances which meant that they could have complete separation of the school and the restaurant. Each floor had high ceilings and large, tall windows that gave a feeling of openness and freedom.

They hugged each other. This was it.

Leslie called Mr. Farrell and asked him to buy the building, arrange all the permits and organize meetings with architects. Then they called Debra and asked if she would help with the plans.

"I want to do the restaurant and cabaret, but not the studios and rehearsal rooms."

Sergei thought this was an interesting proposal because it tripped an idea that had been lurking in the back of his mind. "Okay, and you just reminded me that we can also rent the rehearsal rooms. We can have some for dance and some for vocal or instrument rehearsals."

The first level was for the restaurant and cabaret. The second for administration and the third and fourth for rehearsal studios. The fifth and sixth for studios, changing rooms and instructor breakrooms.

When they had their permits, the work began in earnest. Brian, their architect looked like an offensive tackle or

defensive end told them that when he was a youngster, he'd wanted to take ballet. He said that his six children would be students at the school. For Brian, this was a labor of love and he put his heart and soul into it.

This sort of response was ubiquitous. People answered a call from the heart and for the soul. It wasn't another dance school or restaurant. Theirs was a quest intended to offer unheard of possibilities for children and adults.

* * *

By Spring, the studios were finished. The colors were lavender and warm beige. The floors were sprung. They were buying pianos, and drums for the studios and furniture for the breakrooms and kitchens. The lockers and showers were simple but with adequate space.

When Leslie walked Debra through the two floors of studios, Debra said, "I don't know why or how, but these rooms are soothing. It is lovely but very unusual."

Leslie beamed and suggested they go down to the rehearsal studios. Debra was unusually quiet as they moved from room to room. They had installed the finest in soundproofing so an opera singer could practice with a drummer in the next room. They had decided to give each room a subtle nuance to break the monotony of the typically dull rehearsal studio. Larger rooms had baby grands and

the smaller ones had upright pianos. The colors varied as did the flooring and ceilings. Some of the rooms could be converted into larger or smaller spaces according to need.

Debra kept walking back and forth through each of the rehearsal studios. Finally, she said, "I'm going to start lessons again. I need to do more with my life. Art is the best part of life and I never realized it. You understood that when you were a little girl." Then she burst into tears on their way to the second floor.

Drying her eyes, Debra said, "Anyone working here will be delighted."

The middle area had a kitchen with various kinds of seating and tables. There were straight back chairs, chaises, stools, highchairs. It was suitable for working, eating, taking a nap or meetings. The offices continued the windows concept with glass doors and half glass walls between them. Everyone had privacy as well as freedom.

The first floor was Debra's darling.

"While you were waiting for permits and building, I was talking to everyone I knew. The restaurant was fascinating. The cabaret was complicated in a way.

"There were restaurant owners who declined because of the fear of competition. Others considered it a challenge and a way of advertising. I was thinking about your experience

with the chef in France. I presented it as an opportunity not only to train new chefs but to exhibit their expertise and most of all their love of the art of cuisine. I said they could focus on the artform and that is what ignited them."

Leslie was impressed, "I would never have thought of that."

"I know, I am such a marvel! Anyway, I was taken aback by the number of chefs and sometimes restaurant owners who wanted to emphasize that. Listening to them talk about the art of cooking was an experience. I want that to be embedded in everything we do."

"You have hit the nail on the reason for this mission."

"Because of the overwhelming interest and support, we will be able to keep the prices down. However, it can't be inexpensive. On the other hand, if you and Sergei agree, I would like the cabaret to be like The Carlyle. I should be high end and top of the line.

"We will have performers young and old putting their heart and soul into a performance. I am talking about the hours of practice and literally blood, sweat and tears to offer something moving and memorable. I want the audience to be reminded of that. The dress code will reflect that. Dress elegantly to show respect for those hours of work, frustration and sometimes panic."

Leslie was thinking just as Sergei joined them. They shared Debra's idea with him.

Without hesitation, Sergei said, "That is a perfect idea. I never understood dressing down for any performance. It is disrespectful. As a performer, it is distasteful."

CHAPTER 8
CIRCLE OF LIFE

S ophia was exhausted. She was also happier than she could ever remember. She and Alvaro were engaged, and her father was content.

The evening she told her father about her show, she'd been shaking. She'd been shaking just a trifle less when she requested a leave of absence.

After Alvaro kissed her, she thought they had something to drink, were sitting at a table somewhere, and then he walked her to her train. Because she was floating, she didn't remember much. She did know that she needed to talk to Papa.

They had dinner and were at the table with their coffee when Papa asked, "What do you want to tell me?"

Papa had always been a mind reader. "Papa, I auditioned for a Broadway show and got it. I accepted. On Monday, I will put in a leave of absence from my company."

"How do you feel?"

"Terrified."

"And well you should be! But my baby girl, you must follow our dream. I have felt discontent in you for years, no

matter what you accomplished. Right now, that restlessness isn't there. You are at peace within yourself and with the world."

He paused to sip his coffee. "If you do not do this, the unrest will be back, you will be miserable, and I won't want to be near you. You would not ever forgive yourself and it would gnaw at you.

"Sophia, something that young people can never imagine is that old people were once young."

She threw herself into his arms and they held each other for a long time.

Finally, Sophia said, "There is something else."

She paused, "I met someone today. You must meet him. His name is Alvaro."

Papa started laughing.

"Why are you laughing?" she asked.

"Because you broke open the shell that was containing your life. When you did that, you were able to allow love to happen. You are completely in love and cannot get your sentences out fast enough." He laughed again.

"It's completely obvious. Remember Sophia, I was in love once."

"Do we have any champagne?"

* * *

Alvaro couldn't sleep. He'd been awake all night. His mind was a cauldron. There were three things interrupting his slumber. He planned to marry and have a family with Sophia, he had to talk with the senior partner at S&C, which was unlikely to be a pleasant encounter, and he had to stop supporting his adult family. An additional item was the project with Leslie and Sergei.

On Monday morning, Alvaro went to Ms. Kelly, Mr. Gardner's personal assistant, to set an appointment with him. He was one of the most feared senior partners and had been something of a mentor. He was a tough old curmudgeon and never minced words. He made an appointment for Tuesday at 8:00 and arranged for his assistant to cover for him.

He set up a meeting with his family so that everyone could attend for Monday night.

"Hi guys, I want you to know that I will be changing jobs. I need to do something that makes me happy. I also just met the woman of my dreams and plan to marry her as soon as possible. You will love her too when you meet her."

His father Dinan said, "I want the best for you. We all do."

His mother and siblings were content and undisturbed. He knew they didn't get the ramification of what he was saying.

He continued, "I will be moving out and will not have money to give to you. You are all intelligent and capable and I am sure you can take care of everything yourselves."

They were all still smiling and happy. In that instant, Alvaro decided to find a place the next day. He did not want to be present when they caught on to what was changing.

* * *

Alvaro arrived at the office by 7:30. He'd outlined the salient points of the discussion on the way to work.

He did not want to have this discussion.

Mr. Gardner was a good man, tough, exacting and a master at evaluating situations, things, and people. The rumor was that he'd been a street urchin who shined shoes. A very rich mogul noticed how carefully and beautifully he shined shoes and hired him for his factory. The rest is a story often heard, but not often true. Everywhere, in every job he worked, he excelled and was always studying at night school. Gardner took a fancy to law and was good at it, very good. He liked investing and made a hobby of investment banking. According to Forbes he was one of the

richest men in the country. He caught the eye of S&C, and the rest was history. Even the old boys never crossed him. He'd only had his intelligence, vision and internal power to enable him to forge ahead. Alvaro had always felt a kinship. Perhaps they were both lonely.

By 7:58, Ms. Kelly had announced him, and he was seated before the massive desk by 7:59. Sweating profusely.

"Humph, what is it, Alvaro?"

"I would like to take an extended leave of absence."

Gardner was silent, waiting. He already knew of Alvaro's off-hour work. Indeed, he had made it his business to see him perform, quite a few times. That he was gifted, there was no doubt. Gardner thought he should do something with it.

"I need to feed my soul and will go full time to support myself. If a leave of absence is not feasible, I will offer my resignation."

Gardner looked into Alvaro's eyes for what seemed like an eternity. He truly wished Alvaro were his own son. Wished he had a son.

"Alvaro, you may have the longest LOA possible. If, a very big if, it doesn't work out or isn't what you want, promise me you will let me know directly. I will have you

enrolled in law school full time and then you can return to S&C as an associate."

He opened his top drawer, extracted a book, and began to write. "Take this and this," he said as he put two pieces of paper in an envelope. Then he stood up, walked around his desk and shook Alvaro's hand.

The interview was over, and Alvaro left the office quite dazed. He said his goodbyes to Ms. Kelly and went to the downstairs lounge which he knew would be empty at this time of day.

When he opened the envelope, he was glad that the lounge was empty. One piece of paper had Gardner's home number and a demand to be kept informed. The other was a check for one year's salary.

The emotions that welled in him were undefinable. Dumbfounded came to mind.

CHAPTER 9
CLIMBING

They'd hired seasoned back office personnel for every aspect of administration. They were creating a scholarship system for cleaning, maintenance and reception.

Leslie told everyone about their new space and arranged tours for them to see it. Word spread like wildfire. Studio owners approached her and wanted to bring their student bodies and be part of something magnificent. This meant they could also eliminate exorbitant rentals.

Dancers, dance teachers, choreographers, etc., were artists who worked for the sheer joy of exercising their craft. It was a life without the typical rewards of a typical day job. There were never enough jobs for dancers or instructors with fantastic abilities.

This was why it was possible to hear opera singers, philharmonic musicians, quartets, and choirs performed on subway platforms or streets. They were augmenting their income. As anyone who has every heard them knows, they put their entire beings into each performance.

In a very short time, the studios were open, and classes began. In less than a month, the classes were booked from

morning until evening. There was never a trickle of students, it was an avalanche. They were overjoyed and could now introduce the next two pieces.

Leslie looked and Sergei and said, "I thought we would be at this point in a year. I am amazed."

"That makes two of us. I think it's because we have our hearts in the right place. We did cut ties with a few people who didn't have heart and were out to scrounge or undercut."

"Which should we do first? Our form of the Mickey Mouse Club or the cabaret?" Leslie said.

"Let's focus on the restaurant and the cabaret. By the way, we still don't have a name for either one."

Curious Leslie asked, "Would it be weird to name the restaurant Heart and the cabaret Soul."

Debra had just walked in and joined Sergei in moaning, "Don't even think about such a thing. You focus on the studios and don't try to name anything. Orlov and Beaumont into The ORB for the studio was brilliant, but clearly that was the end of your genius."

Feeling somewhat crushed that her brilliant idea was trashed, Leslie adjusted and continued, "Debra, what have you conjured up for the cuisine? How many chefs do you have now?"

"I have been intrigued because the chefs like voting and competition so much. I have been considering ways of doing that in a way that is elegant. This what I have produced so far. Please add on, delete or tell me how fabulous I am."

Leslie groaned and Sergei covered his eyes.

"Lunch will be a regular enterprise. Standards and staples with an expanded number of vegan and vegetarian dishes." Debra took a deep breath.

"The incomparable Culinary Art Pursuit may be purchased with four, eight or twelve dinners a month. We will also take drop-ins and reservations. Gentlemen will wear suits, or jackets and ties, and ladies should be in cocktail wear or short formals. I am courting every well-known clothes designer in the City to come for dinner and will have the photographers here as well. We'll have to feed them of course.

"For those patrons who are doing our Culinary Art Pursuit, they will be able to choose their favorite cuisine. They will be asked to evaluate their dinners. I am also wooing members of all the boards I am on and all committee members I know." Debra petered out.

"I like it because it's unique and has a certain cachet that is appealing. Being in a gorgeous venue with A-listers is enough."

"Sergei, I agree with you. The clientele we want can have anything they want. It is important that we lure them in, and we can up the ante or twist it or change it to keep them very interested. Our main objective is to have a place for chefs to develop and create. It's also an exceptional opportunity for prospective restaurateurs to learn the ropes. They can have an apprenticeship like the chefs. This is so exciting."

Debra said softly, "So you like it?"

"Yes, silly!"

"It's brilliant," Sergei agreed. "It's going to be complicated and frustrating and infinitely rewarding. When is the unveiling? I tried to sneak down there last week and was given the bum's rush."

"Would tomorrow morning at 6:00am work for you?"

They both nodded.

* * *

They could see her from half a block away. Debra was standing outside moving from one foot to the other.

Leslie said, "I've never seen her so on edge before."

With a shrug, Sergei said, "It is odd."

When she saw them, she ran and put her arms around them and practically dragged them through the carved

doors. Once they entered, all evidence of simplicity was gone.

Debra had taken full advantage of the sixteen foot ceilings by installing slim pillars every ten feet that were etched with faux foliage which continued across the arches between them. She'd created an illusion with entwined chandeliers that gave the feeling of an old European castle. She'd chosen royal blue, gold and deep wine for her color scheme. The floor was a dark, rich brown stone. She'd built several enormous fireplaces as focal points. The tables were a discrete distance from each other, and the linen, china and cutlery were perfect. The restrooms were spacious, elegant and full of fragrant plants.

"Debra, you have outdone yourself."

"This is second to none. I love it."

"I went through every magazine I could and talked with the chefs. The place had to be beautiful, welcoming and convenient for movement for the servers. I really didn't have anything to do with the kitchens and their setup. Frankly, I still don't understand how it works. Since ten different chefs raved about it, I am on board."

＊ ＊ ＊

"We aren't done yet. Come on. To reach the cabaret, we go through this fun tunnel. It is like a priests' hold entrance

that widens into an entrancing tunnel. People like fun things. Push this book and the door slides in. The distance also serves as a buffer to prevent sound from infiltrating either space. Patrons could also gain entrance from the street if they had not had dinner.

The transformation was complete. It was as though they had entered both a space and a time warp.

The ambiance was subdued medieval. It could play to jazz, opera, Broadway or cabaret. It was intimate, close and easy. Debra demonstrated how the lights could be adjusted to change the look and feel of the space. It was superb, divine, and wonderful.

They thanked Debra. "I had been afraid you wouldn't like it. I couldn't sleep last night."

"Debra, it is amazing and so are you. I had no idea of the depths of my little sister's talents."

"I am thinking what else we can turn you loose on to work your magic." Sergei said. "If you can think of anything you would like to see done, let us know. You have a rare talent."

Debra was smiling and looked like she was just about to cry. In a small voice, she said, "Thank you. I wanted you to like it. This is so important. This is where they will do their 'American Idol' auditions. Right here!

Sergei was enraptured, "I think we ought to have a bio, or back story that we can hand out so that people know who they are. We'll be creating an entirely new world for singers. And it won't be geared toward fame and fortune. It'll be about soul."

CHAPTER 10
LIFTOFF

L eslie had just finished a conversation about creating their concept of a vehicle to launch the youngsters.

She said, "I think we should create our own template."

Sergei nodded and asked, "What do you have in mind?"

"I was afraid you'd ask me that." She paused to gather her thoughts and said, "Everything we are doing is for exposing talent. We have a dance school with a unique mission. Our restaurant will become a nurturing center and produce superior chefs. By the way, Debra was talking about bringing chefs from Italy, France, Mexico, and Africa to train here for six months.

This one is for younger people. They will have training in dance, voice, acting and any other gift we discover in them. They will do solo and ensemble performances in some way, somewhere once a week.

"This would be preparation for major tours in the summers, nationwide or internationally. During the school year, they'd only perform on weekends in nearby venues like the Jersey Shore or Upstate New York."

"That is very comprehensive. Someone here would coordinate parental permissions, chaperones and all the

other minutiae. This will take some time to implement. What is your targeted start date?"

"This will be intricate because of the underage complications, elements of schooling and having parents underfoot all the time. Oh, something I thought of is that the kids' first performances should be for their parents, relatives, and friends.

"We are focusing on bringing out the soul and showing the gifts that they possess. I imagine a lot of these kids have been put down for being silly or useless because they want to dance, sing or act. It's no secret that if one person tells another one person something cannot be done, not to do it, or laughs at it, that person is often afraid to do anything himself. That is the reason I want he first performances to be for these people."

"I'm with you on that. Just like with the body, emotions can sometimes prevent a gift from manifesting itself. This is out job and our mission. What goals do you have for these kids."

"After they go through our program, they will have solid experience performing in dance, voice and acting, as soloists and in an ensemble or chorus. Because of their in-depth study, they will be able to knowledgeably choose a path that is right for them. Alternatively, it could lead to the discovery that performance is not for them at all.

"It could be that they prefer doing makeup, staging, directing, or lighting. There are so many elements that go into any performance."

"I think songwriting and scriptwriting should be added to their curriculum."

"That's a terrific idea. I hadn't thought of it. It is perfect and fleshes out everything else that they'll be doing. They have to study music and we can augment it with the songwriting. The idea of scriptwriting is sheer genius. They will be taking acting classes and scriptwriting is a perfect way to enhance the craft."

"You said that Sophia had studied the old movies and history of the theater. We have video capability in the larger rooms. Seeing oneself is sometimes as good as receiving pages of notes. We can make copies of the videos and for them to study. We certainly have the capability of making a few movies in the meantime."

"Sergei, where is this going? You are bursting with ideas."

"The sky is the limit. Maybe, we should say that the moon is the limit. At least for now."

* * *

Sophia believed that performing was more challenging than any job she had ever had or could even imagine.

No mistakes. No excuses.

Every performance had to be executed with precision, energy, power and exuberance. No audience wanted to pay for a lackluster show.

Sophia loved every aspect of what she was doing. She could not explain the feeling of exultation she had when she was giving everything that was inside of her.

The rehearsals were more intense than the audition. At one point, she sensed her annoyance because of the constant repetition of a part that everyone knew well. In the next few repetitions, Sophia's dancing went onto another level, she hadn't thought possible. From then on, she looked forward to breaking through boundaries. She realized that boundaries were self-made. Then, she understood. She looked up and met the eyes of the choreographer. He smiled. He knew what had happened to her. He crafted a solo for her. Her dancing became even more explosive.

* * *

After rehearsals, all she could do was get on the subway, try not to sleep past her stop and get home to kiss her father and fall into bed. Sleep was instant.

When she worked for the electric company and the advertising firm, Sophia thought it was demanding work.

Now it seemed like no work at all. What was chilling was that looking back, it seemed like she had been half alive. There had been no power or energy in her life.

There was a live current in her life now and for that she loved every sore muscle and every sore toe. Her life was on fire, and she was doing what she was born to do.

She spoke with Alvaro every day.

* * *

Alvaro immediately phoned a rental agency and took a month to month rental on a furnished apartment at West End Avenue and 64th Street. He'd returned home to pack and within an hour had all he needed. He would not be back.

Then he'd contacted Leslie and shared his experience with Mr. Gardner. In the middle of a sentence, Leslie said, "I'll call you back." And was gone.

Alvaro went back to organizing his studio apartment. He knew it was temporary because he would need a larger place for his future bride. I reminisced at how his life had moved swiftly since he met Leslie. Perhaps it was because he had committed his life to his dream. He felt strong.

The phone rang and it was Leslie, "Hi Alvaro, there are two things we should talk over. Do you have time today?"

He laughed and said, "I am no longer employed. What time is good for you?"

"How about 5:00 and we could do dinner as well. Let's meet at Sergei's place." And gave him the address.

Happily, Alvaro continued organizing his meager space. He had about an hour before they met. He made of his bed and double-checked he had all his toiletries and made a list of groceries he would need.

He started his walk to Sergei's apartment. He loved the old buildings on the west side because they had so much character.

When he arrived, they both met him at the door and looked suspiciously like they had just devoured a canary.

When they were settled with Compari and sodas, Sergei opened with, "We have been reviewing every aspect of our project and it is going well. We don't have enough hands or feet." He looked at Leslie. "Leslie told me about your exciting changes, and I would like to offer my congratulations. I would also like to offer you a new position."

"We need more men's teachers and at the same time, we specifically need someone with more breakdancing, and hip-hop technique. You are perfect for a host of reasons, not the least of which is that you have so much passion."

Alvaro couldn't contain himself and jumped up and said, "Of course, I couldn't ask for a better opportunity. There are no coincidences."

Leslie continued, "Would you also be part of our planning, input and all?"

"Of course." He plopped back down on the sofa, "I really think this is a dream!"

"I know we are asking a lot, but we are getting married shortly and I won't need this apartment anymore. Would you like to have it?"

Alvaro said, "It is a dream."

"I bought it a long time ago, so the rent is a tremendous bargain. It's probably less than your rental. Come on, let me show you." They left to go to the other rooms.

Leslie proceeded to put the finishing touches on their dinner. It was risotto with truffles their favorite and she suspected it would soon be a favorite of Alvaro's as well.

Sergei said, "It has two large bedrooms. I sleep in the smaller one and the master bedroom is setup with barres, mirrors and a great floor for practicing jumps."

"I am sold," said Alvaro. "Nothing could be more perfect. I love the views and the spaciousness. Thank you."

As they returned to the dining room, Sergei said, "You have a little more to do. For our wedding, we want you as best man, Debra as maid of honor and Sophia as bridesmaid. The wedding will be small, but we need to choose a date when Sophia can come. Would you let us know. The sooner the better. This weekend? We already have our marriage license."

"This may seem odd, but if you don't mind, I would like to invite Mr. Gardner, my surrogate father. I want you to all know each other. This seems like the perfect time."

"Let's do it."

Leslie said, "I would like Sophia to bring her father as well, if he has time. Your fathers are very important people and integral to everything we are doing." And it was settled.

Sophia told Alvaro that her father would be delighted and that the upcoming weekend was an excellent choice. She just had to find time to shop for a dress.

Leslie called her immediately, "Sophia you don't need to shop because we are all about the same size. You can choose something from my wardrobe or Debra could bring some dresses down. What's your shoe size?"

"That would be perfect. You know there is no time and I do want to look lovely for your wedding. Papa is

dying to meet you. He already pulled his old tuxedo out of mothballs. He lost so much weight after Mama died that I think he will be able to fit in it again."

* * *

Alvaro took a deep breath and called Mr. Gardner. He answered immediately.

"Hello Mr. Gardner, this is Alvaro. I have so much to tell you and I want to invite you to a wedding this weekend. Not mine, the people I am working with."

"I will come to the wedding. Let's meet for dinner and you can tell me everything. Tomorrow at 6:00 at the Atlantic Grill. Ms. Kelly will make reservations."

"Yes, thank you."

When he rang off, Alvaro exhaled and sat there unable to move.

* * *

Alvaro arrived early as was his wont. He was sipping water, planning and wondering what he was doing here for dinner with one of the richest and most powerful men in the City. He would find out.

He saw him. Mr. Gardner looked wonderful. He was wearing a less formal suit, but Alvaro knew it cost five

grand. His walk was lighter, and his normally rocklike face looked almost relaxed.

"Good evening, Mr. Gardner," said Alvaro standing.

"Sit down, Alvaro, my name is Brad."

"Hello, Brad," said Alvaro as he took his seat again.

"Thank you for coming, I am really glad we could meet." He took a sip of water.

"They already know my order, so please take a moment to look at the menu."

"I got here early so I am all set."

Brad said, "Please tell me everything and leave nothing out. Then I will tell you everything."

And Alvaro did. He was happy to share his story because it was so rarely that he felt able to do so.

They ate and drank as Alvaro took Brad through his awakenings with Baryshnikov, his discovery of ballet, and the passions that were unleashed. He told him about taking care of his family and relatives, and how he had feared following his dream because of those responsibilities. He told him about that elusive dimension that he couldn't seem to reach. He described his first meeting with Leslie, and later with Sergei and Sophia.

He paused as he explained, "Sophia and I plan to marry. She is the loveliest woman in the world, and I fell in love with her the instant I laid eyes on her. You'll meet her on Saturday. I will let her tell you her own story.

"Within four days, I decided to stop supporting my family and relatives, try for a LOA with the firm, and move out of my house. Though I had explained to my family that I was changing my job and wouldn't be their bank anymore, I could see in their eyes that they didn't expect there to be any change whatsoever. I knew I had to get out. I rented a furnished place not too far from here.

"I called to invite you to the wedding because it is important to me that you know these people. They are people like you. But I'm getting ahead of myself.

"I phoned Leslie to give her an update. She practically hung up on me and then called back and invited me to dinner. I learned that they are getting married, wanted me to be best man and Sergei offered me his apartment. I wanted you to know this."

They were on coffee and port by this time.

Brad said, "Alvaro, you are an amazing young man. I could see things in you when you joined the firm five years ago. That is why you got the offer for a free ride. I am glad that you turned it down. What you are doing is infinitely better.

"My father was a brilliant tax attorney with a CPA, He had worked for the IRS on very large cases. I was the only boy with three sisters. It was a nice life he gambled everything away. It was harsh. My mother remained in denial until her death from breast cancer. Two of my sisters are alcoholics and the third is a nun.

"I left home, had to fend for myself and worked myself to the bone. It was rough for a long time. I read a lot and was surprised to discover that I love law. I also love investment banking and it was touch and go for a while because I didn't know which direction to take. I opted for law, but investment banking is still my hobby.

"I allow people to teach me everything. I rarely ask questions because I do not need to. People always tell you with body language, what they watch, their tone of voice. It's old hat now but is still interesting. I know that most people are not happy. In fact, most of them are rather miserable. They think having a lot of money will make them happy. They are quite wrong.

"I am forty-five and planning to retire this year or the next. I envy you because you are pursuing your dream. I do wish I had found something with soul when I was a lad."

They were both silent; they understood each other on a level that few people ever reach.

Brad called for the bill and Alvaro reached for it. Brad said, "I appreciate your gesture and applaud you for making it. Thank you, but no. You have made my day in many ways."

As they parted at the door, Brad smiled and said, " See you on Saturday."

Alvaro had never seen him smile. He was a handsome gentleman.

CHAPTER 11

SOUL

Papa called, "How do I look?"

When Sophia looked at her father, she could barely speak. "Papa, you look dashing. And will turn the head of every woman in the place."

Papa's face turned quite red, and he ducked his head. "You are smashing in that dress. Is it new?"

"I had no time to shop so I borrowed it from the bride." She grimaced, "The shoes are gorgeous, but my feet are already killing me. Ready?"

* * *

Alvaro arrived at the small church on West 78th Street very early. He couldn't wait to see Sophia. Though they talked as much as they could, he hadn't seen her in six days. He was overjoyed at her success and had practically hit the ceiling when she told him about her solo.

He also couldn't wait for Sophia, Bradley, Sergei and Leslie to meet each other. There were butterflies in his stomach.

* * *

Debra was divine in her elegant silk suit. She was making sure that she and Leslie left on time.

Leslie was perfect. The forties theme mirrored the elegance and gentility of her life.

"Come on, get a move on, you don't want the groom to give up on you and leave."

* * *

Brad decided to where a tuxedo that he hadn't worn since he made partner. He was dapper.

On his way out, he dabbed on a bit of cologne.

* * *

Sergei was the happiest he had ever been in his life and couldn't wait to be married.

* * *

The small church was a perfect setting. The groom and his best man waited at the altar.

Two guests attended, Papa and Brad. Seated beside each other there was an uncanny similarity between them.

The music began and Sophia walked gracefully down the aisle. Brad was happy for Alvaro. But then when Debra began her walk, something moved in the pit of his stomach. Who was she? He tried not to stare and turned to see the

loveliest bride. So, this was Leslie. Anyone could feel her power. He thought she was amazing.

Her groom was a perfect match for her.

The ceremony was short, and everyone got into the waiting limousine and proceeded to a reception at Leonti's.

Though not everyone had met before, the group was like a family. Brad asked Sophia to share her story with him.

Sergei said to Leslie, "Have you noticed anything?"

"Of course," she said, "Maybe we should change the name of our restaurant and school to "Love is in the Air."

"It is uncanny."

Alvaro whispered to Sophia, "Were we like that?"

"From what Leslie and Sergei said, we were. I guarantee that if there were an explosion of fireworks, they wouldn't notice a thing."

"They seem perfect."

* * *

By the end of the year, The ORB was a household name in the theatrical world and the touring companies had garnered rave reviews.

Every week another famous instructor would phone and ask to collaborate with them. They were always seeking to

improve, augment, and inspire. Their dream continued to expand but their message remained the same.

The Epicurean Restaurant was on reservations only out to three months.

Le Cabaret was a phenomenal success. Patrons loved the ambiance and how it could change according to the singer or type of music.

* * *

Sophia's show had its run extended by four months. There was discussion about its going on a national tour. Her spectacular dancing had won fabulous praise, but when journalists discovered that she had begun dancing in her twenties, she became an overnight celebrity. She'd been on talk shows, been the main topic in magazines and had done seminars.

Her message was clear and magnificent, and everyone could relate to it. She emphasized how terrified she had been in the beginning, and how challenging the work was. She was also clear about the fact that the reward of doing what she loved every day was worth everything to her.

Alvaro and Sophia had encouraged Papa to collaborate with the company and move to Manhattan. He wanted his own place, so they found an apartment for him in Leslie

and Sergio's building. He was initially skeptical but grew to loved Riverside Drive. He became a florist. They learned that among farmers in Italy, gardening was a natural thing.

Alvaro too had been interviewed by various magazines because his performances had been lauded. It was some time before they registered that his and Sophia's message was the same. Alvaro was teaching, performing and taking classes in every genre he could. He and Sergei had discussions about taking a step into a downsized Cirque du Soleil in the Cabaret. They both loved the concept and knew it would require about a year to mount it. Gymnastics, dance and singing all wrapped into one. The theme had to be Soul, that each of us designed to do something unique.

Leslie was fascinated watching Debra and Brad act like teenagers. It was perfectly wonderful. Brad had retired after his second date with Debra. He asked if he could work for the company and was willing to do anything except dance or sing.

He confided to Debra that he wished that he had a son like Alvaro. He thought he was the finest young man he had every met. He had so much dignity, shouldered responsibility and was gentle and courageous.

Debra had scuttled plans to author a book about gold-diggers. It no longer held any interest. When they first met,

they would share gold-digger stories. They both felt that people like that had no ability to live fully. Her happiness with Brad was beyond anything she could have imagined. She loved everything about him. He was indebted to Alvaro because it was through his invitation to Leslie and Sergei's wedding that he had met Debra.

* * *

Leslie and Sergei were delighted with what they had achieved. Together they were inseparable, balanced and powerful. Their individual trauma had made them stronger individually and as a couple.

The right people had been drawn to them as soon as they decided what they wanted to do. They made a concrete determination, and the effect was that Alvaro, Sophia, Debra had all stepped in. They still giggled about Alvaro and Sophia, but even more about Debra and Brad.

Debra had stepped up to the plate for the first time that Leslie knew. Brad had taken a deep interest in Alvaro and Alvaro invited him as his surrogate father.

Sergei still complained that Riverside Drive was too far away from Fairway. Nonetheless, he was exceedingly happy.

Leslie often thought of her mother because she was the key to everything. She had constantly taken her two darlings

into Manhattan, and it was from those visits that Leslie had become a ballerina. She met Sergei, the injury and recovery and her rebirth. The rest is history.

She said, "Sergei, do you want children?"

"Not necessarily. Do you?"

"No. I don't think the world right is any kind of place bring a child. What we are doing is something that can put a dent in the lethargy and apathy. But we are far from having something worthwhile to offer a child."

"You are right. We do have our 'baby' though. Our project is our baby."

MANNY CABO

Every once in a while, in the ever competitive entertainment industry, a presence enters the scene that turns heads, opens eyes and ears, touches hearts and makes a lasting impact on everyone they encounter: Such is the case with the multifaceted, Commercial Rockin, arts-embracing and award winning Singer / Songwriter Manny Cabo. From his incredible 4 chair turn on NBC's "THE VOICE" and recently mirroring his vocal prowess and breaking linguistic boundaries on NBC / Telemundo's "LA VOZ." Cabo has been leaving his creative mark and vocal resonance on an international level and across multi cultural boundaries. Whether he's singing, acting, photographing, or hosting, his compelling focus and his artistry shines through and always leaves his fans and clients wanting more.

- Owner of Manny Cabo Media LLC
- Received 4-chair turn on NBC's *The Voice* for Team Adam Levine, Season 9
- First NJ Artist to perform on two major network competitions bilingually 2015, 2019
- Rock Entertainer of the Year 2017 (JM Awards) Nashville, TN
- Unsigned artist song of the year for "90 Proof" (WOBA Awards) Nashville, TN
- Best Music / Editorial Photographer of the year 2016, 2017, 2018
- Performed a five sold-out arena tour with American Young Voices 2017
- Awarded Seal of Elizabeth award by Elizabeth Mayor 2016
- Unsigned Rock Entertainer of the Year (JM Awards) Nashville, TN
- Humanitarian award for his anti-hate song "Hate Has No Home Here"
- Featured artist on *PATCH* magazine for his anti-bullying song "Wear Your Words"
- Featured on Telemundo's *La Voz* for seven-time Grammy award winner Carlos Vives
- Endorsed by Sennheiser, Westone, Photoflex, Quantum, Dynalite, Hoodman & Thalia

- Performed as featured rock artist on *Today in Nashville* 2016, 2018
- Performed as opener for: 3 Doors Down, Lifehouse, Cold, John Waite, SR71 & more
- Artist of the month feature for top NJ Music Magazine *The Aquarian* 2019
- Over 15 million you tube views for *The Voice, La Voz* and his *Mojo For Musicians* channel
- 25,000 loyal fan base following across all social media platforms
- Advisory Board member for *Power Me Up Radio Talk* on iHeart
- Executive Producer and Host for Top 15 Music Podcast *Mojo for Musicians*
- Lead vocalist for the Wizards of Winter
- Voted the sexiest voice on ClubHouse in 2021

Management / M.C.MEDIA LLC
Booking / Nigel Ratcliffe, info@mannycabo.com, 908.239.4713
Press / Nigel Ratcliffe, 615.967.4600

www.mannycabo.com

MORE ACCOLADES FOR MANNY

"I absolutely loved being on your show Manny. You are a true professional and a complete rock star in everything that you do, and I appreciate all that you're doing for the music community."

Kelly Sutton – Emmy Winning TV Host / Personality

"Speaking with Manny and joining him on his podcast journey was extremely refreshing. He asked the right questions and knew how to engage in heartfelt dialogue which is so important in building relationships. His passion for living, creating, and inspiring is truly contagious."

Forbes Riley – CEO & Creator of Spin Gym, TV Health / Fitness Celebrity

CPSIA information can be obtained
at www.ICGtesting.com
Printed in the USA
BVHW021814150622
639898BV00005B/55